P9-DMC-124

Ellen's Broom

KELLY STARLING LYONS

illustrated by DANIEL MINTER

G. P. PUTNAM'S SONS • AN IMPRINT OF PENGUIN GROUP (USA) INC.

DISCARDED
from
New Hanover County Public Library

NEW HANOVER COUNTY PUBLIC LIBRARY
201 Chestnut Street
Wilmington, N.C. 28401

G. P. PUTNAM'S SONS

A division of Penguin Young Readers Group.
Published by The Penguin Group.
Penguin Group (USA) Inc., 375 Hudson Street, New York, NY 10014, U.S.A.
Penguin Group (Canada), 90 Eglinton Avenue East, Suite 700, Toronto, Ontario M4P 2Y3, Canada
(a division of Pearson Penguin Canada Inc.).
Penguin Books Ltd, 80 Strand, London WC2R 0RL, England.
Penguin Ireland, 25 St. Stephen's Green, Dublin 2, Ireland (a division of Penguin Books Ltd.).
Penguin Group (Australia), 250 Camberwell Road, Camberwell, Victoria 3124, Australia
(a division of Pearson Australia Group Pty Ltd).
Penguin Books India Pvt Ltd, 11 Community Centre, Panchsheel Park, New Delhi - 110 017, India.
Penguin Group (NZ), 67 Apollo Drive, Rosedale, Auckland 0632, New Zealand
(a division of Pearson New Zealand Ltd).
Penguin Books (South Africa) (Pty) Ltd, 24 Sturdee Avenue, Rosebank, Johannesburg 2196, South Africa.
Penguin Books Ltd, Registered Offices: 80 Strand, London WC2R 0RL, England.

Text copyright © 2012 by Kelly Starling Lyons.
Illustrations copyright © 2012 by Daniel Minter.
All rights reserved. This book, or parts thereof, may not be reproduced in any form without
permission in writing from the publisher, G. P. Putnam's Sons, a division of Penguin Young Readers Group,
345 Hudson Street, New York, NY 10014. G. P. Putnam's Sons, Reg. U.S. Pat. & Tm. Off.
The scanning, uploading and distribution of this book via the Internet or via any other means without
the permission of the publisher is illegal and punishable by law. Please purchase only authorized
electronic editions, and do not participate in or encourage electronic piracy of copyrighted materials.
Your support of the author's rights is appreciated. The publisher does not have any control over and
does not assume any responsibility for author or third-party websites or their content.
Published simultaneously in Canada.
Manufactured in China by South China Printing Co. Ltd.

Design by Ryan Thomann.
Text set in Cheltenham ITC Book Condensed.
The art was created from linoleum block prints that were printed by hand and painted.

Library of Congress Cataloging-in-Publication Data is available upon request.
ISBN 978-0-399-25003-3
1 3 5 7 9 10 8 6 4 2

For Patrick, Jordan and Joshua, our loving families,
and all of the ancestors who paved the way.
—K.S.L.

To Marcia.
—D.M.

Sunday morning, Ellen sat on the front pew with her family. She wiggled on the wooden seat, trying to get comfortable. But she knew not to say a word. Her people no longer had to worship at the back of the master's church or sneak to the woods for prayer meetings. Slavery days were over. They had so much to be thankful for.

Ellen heard something new in the voices that swelled the church, built by her own, with song. They were free! Joy filled her heart.

Just then, Deacon stood to speak. He clutched a paper and raised it to heaven.

"To God be the glory," he roared. "All former slaves living as husband and wife shall be registered and seen as married in the eyes of the law."

All over the church, people leapt to their feet. Ellen did too. She understood only a little of what the preacher said. But she knew it was good. Her mother's eyes brimmed with tears. Her papa's hands clapped like thunder.

Back home in their cabin, Ellen's parents walked over to the broom hanging on the wall. Mama always said it was part of the family—a witness to the way things were. She told the broom story over and over so they would never forget what they survived. "Ruby and Ruben," Mama asked the twins, "do you know what this broom was for?"

"Weddings, Mama," Ruben answered quickly.

"That's right," Mama said, nodding. "Broom weddings were all most slaves were allowed to have."

"Before freedom came, the law wasn't on our side," Papa told them. "Husbands and wives could be ripped apart, sold away at any time. It didn't matter if they cried or even begged to stay together. Master had the final say."

As Ellen thought about her parents' words, she tried to imagine life without them. Her eyes burned and her heart ached.

"That's not right," she said, shaking her head and trying to clear the image from her mind.

"But we did the best we could with what we had," Papa said. "Deacon said a few words. Then we put this here broom on the ground, held hands and leaped into life together."

"We were married in our hearts and in God's eyes," Mama said. "But we had no way to show it. That's all changed now. We can be married legal just like anybody else."

A couple weeks later, when the sun peeked its rosy head into the sky, Mama said it was time for the journey. Ellen washed and dressed quickly. Ruby grinned and carried baby Noah on her hip. Ruben toted a sack with food. Mama took down the broom and handed it to Ellen.

"This broom was there from the start. So it should come
along too, don't you think?" she said with a wink.

Ellen felt her chest puff with pride. She smiled and
clutched the broom tight.

As they walked to the courthouse, people from church, going for the same reason, joined them. Ellen looked around at the parade of strutting families and her parents holding hands. She listened to the sweet laughter and songs sailing in the air. She held the broom high.

They stopped at a beautiful building near a row of flowers. Papa bowed his head and gave thanks that they arrived safely.

Ellen's eyes grew large as they stepped inside. A Freedmen's Bureau officer interviewed a couple in the line in front of them. He wrote the man's and lady's names on a special register. Ruby said they were already married, but being part of that record was proof that they were legal husband and wife.

Ellen looked at the woman's pretty dress and at her mama's plain one made of homespun cotton. She grabbed Ruby's arm and hurried her out of the room.

"Where are you taking me, Ellen?" her big sister asked.

"I have an idea," Ellen said as her eyes twinkled. "Did you see that patch of flowers outside?"

Ruby nodded and a smile stretched across her face.

The sisters ran out and carefully plucked some flowers. Then they weaved them through the straw until the broom was decorated with blooms of red and pink.

In the courthouse, Ellen handed the broom to Mama, flower side up. Her mother's eyes filled with tears.

"What's wrong, Mama?" Ellen asked, worried she had done something bad.

"Nothing, baby," she said. "Everything is just right."

The man added Papa's and Mama's names to the register. Then he asked them for the year they started living together as husband and wife and the names and ages of their children. Ellen grinned when Papa said hers.

When the man finished writing, he explained that Mama and Papa were married in the eyes of God and the law. He handed them a certificate to take home. Papa kissed Mama and whirled her in the air like a new bride.

On the way home, the family stopped for lunch beneath a shade tree.
Ellen picked up the broom and laid it in front of her parents.

"I want to see you jump the broom. Please? Can you?"

Papa frowned. "Broom jumping is the past, Lil Bit. We're married, official."

"Please, Papa," Ellen said. "Mama always says the broom is part of us too."

"Papa's right," Mama said. "The broom is the past."

Ellen hung her head.

"But you're right too," Mama said. "It will always be part of who we are.
Come on, Papa. Let's show these young folks how it's done."

"When I get married one day, I'm going to jump the broom too," Ellen said suddenly. Papa hesitated, then grinned.

"That would be mighty fine, Lil Bit," he said. "Mighty fine."

When they returned to their cabin, Mama looked at the bare wall and then at Ellen.

"That wall sure could use some fixing up," she said.

Ellen knew just what it needed. As the last rays of light warmed the room, she smiled and hung up the certificate and the broom together.

AUTHOR'S NOTE

Growing up in Pittsburgh, my family taught me to honor history. I felt a rush when I moved to North Carolina and realized a part of my heritage was just a drive away. My maternal granddad's people, the Hairstons and Starlings, carved out a life in Eden, NC, and nearby Virginia counties. One weekend, my husband and I spent hours in a Rockingham County library's genealogy room.

It was there that I discovered the document that inspired this story—the 1866 Cohabitation List of Henry County, Virginia. That list was necessary, because of an injustice: Slave marriages were not protected by law. At any time, slaveholders could sell husbands and wives, parents and children away from each other. After slavery ended, some African Americans searched heartbroken for loved ones. But for some couples, freedom brought a right they had been denied. During Reconstruction, the marriages of former slaves were made legal. Often, Freedmen's Bureau officers registered the couples. Sometimes they even issued marriage certificates. For the first time, many African Americans had proof that their sacred unions were recognized by law.

In my fictional story inspired by history, Ellen brought the broom on the journey to the courthouse as a link to the past. Her family remembered what they survived even as they celebrated the promise of the future. Today, some African Americans broom jump at their weddings in memory of that history. My husband and I still have our broom decorated with cowry shells and silk flowers. It's a symbol of our commitment and a tie to the trials our people have overcome.

This book would not have been possible without the help and support of my family and friends; National Archives and Records Administration African American genealogy specialist Reginald Washington; author Eleanora E. Tate and professor Dr. Pauletta Bracy; the Writers Workshop at Chautauqua; curator Earl Ijames and youth and family programs coordinator Emily Grant of the NC Museum of History; Gregory Tyler, curatorial consultant for Historic Hope Plantation; United Arts Council of Raleigh & Wake County; Madison Library in Madison, NC; Bassett Historical Center in Bassett, Virginia; and the Virginia Center for Digital History's Valley of the Shadow Project.

I am also deeply grateful to editors Nancy Paulsen and Stacey Barney, agents Jeff Dwyer and Elizabeth O'Grady, and illustrator Daniel Minter for believing in this story and bringing it to life.

MLib

6/12